# Daisy
## and the Diva

ALAN FRASER
ILLUSTRATED BY MELANIE SHARP

# Chapter 1
## Mrs Bun and Dr Bones

"So why can't Mrs Bun run off with Dr Bones?"

"Because those aren't the rules!" said Meggy. "Card games do have rules you know."

"I know … but so what? We could change

them. I mean, Mrs Bun could run off with Dr Bones and Mrs Bones could run off with Dr Dose. And Mrs Dose ..."

Well, that was enough for Meggy. "Daisy!" she said. "It's not a TV soap! It's called *Happy Families*!"

"I know it is," I said. "But, well ... we could change that too, couldn't we?"

"You're mad!"

"But we should keep all the names," I added. I really liked the names, and the little pictures. There was Mr Snip the tailor, and Mrs Dip the dyer's wife, and Miss Chip the carpenter's daughter. And you can guess what Master Bun got up to.

"You know what?" I said. "Barry's mum could be in *Happy Families*, couldn't she?"

Barry was in our class at school.

"What?" said Meggy. "Mrs Clinkscales?"

"Exactly! She'd be Mrs Clinkscales the piano teacher!"

Mrs Clinkscales came into school on Tuesdays and bashed away at the piano while we sang our songs. They were fun, too, but they weren't the sort of songs you ever heard on the radio.

Mrs Clinkscales, the piano teacher.

Cool.

It was Friday assembly, Miss Melrose was strumming her guitar and the whole school was singing. We were making a good noise, too.

Standing out front – like he always does – was Mr Pollard. He's our headteacher. We call him Polly. He was keeping a close eye on us, because that morning we had a guest to impress. Sitting up on stage was a man a bit younger than my dad, with a soppy smile plastered on his face.

I waited until we finished off the song,

then I gave Meggy a nudge. "Who's that?" I whispered.

"Dunno," she mouthed at me.

Well, we soon found out.

"Right children," said Polly. "I want to introduce you to Harvey Butterworth."

So this was the man with the soppy smile – Harvey Butterworth.

Polly went on. "Mr Butterworth is a well-known composer of music, and, luckily for Flittering, he's been asked to write a community opera for the town festival. But, the best part is ... he wants our school choir to be part of the opera!"

Wow, I thought. Our school choir in an opera! I mean, cool! At least it would've been – except for one tiny thing. So I stuck up my hand.

"But Sir ... we haven't got a school choir."

Polly chuckled nervously. "Yes, thank you, Daisy," he said. "Not a regular choir maybe.

But hearing you all sing this morning I'm sure Mr Butterworth is ... er ... um ... er ..."

Well, just in time, Harvey Butterworth gave Polly a little smiley nod, so he stopped looking all flustered.

"Anyway," Polly told us, "there'll be a letter going home about the opera with Years Five and Six."

Wow, I thought. I was in Year Five, so that meant me!

"D'you think there'll be a great big lady who dies at the end?"

We were in the playground talking about the opera.

"Could be," said Meggy. "That happens a lot in opera doesn't it? I think she's called a diva."

Then Ravi had a suggestion. "Maybe a warrior with a magic sword will save the world from some evil wizard?"

We ignored that.

"And they could have long spears," said Ravi, "and cow horns on their helmets."

Well, that's when I asked the question. "Has anyone we know actually been to an opera?"

No one had.

Miss Melrose gave out the letters at the end of school, and by the time we got to the gates, Meggy and I had read ours.

Twice.

Meggy's mum met us that day.

"Goodness," she said, "you two look excited!"

Meggy gave her mum the letter. "Guess what?" Meggy said. "There's going to be an opera."

"And we can be in it," I added. "Years Five

8

and Six are making a choir."

"The opera's called *Constant Billy*."

"But we don't know what it's about. Not yet."

Meggy's mum had a look at the letter. "Goodness!" she said. "How interesting!"

And it was, too.

My brother wasn't impressed. Surprise, surprise!

"Opera's boring!"

"No it's not," I said – like I was the big expert. "You're just jealous!"

"In your dreams," he muttered. "I'd rather stick my head down the toilet and blow bubbles."

"Okay. I'll help you!"

"All right you two!" said Mum. "That's quite enough."

"Well, Jamie's being horrible," I said.

Then I heard Dad come in. So I grabbed the letter and ran to show him.

# Chapter 2
## Constant Billy

Well, from what I could see, the school choir was going to be the whole of Year Five and the whole of Year Six, because everyone was up for it. Even Jimmy Black brought in his slip, and that's practically a miracle.

Polly made an announcement at assembly. "And I'm sure you'll be a credit to the school," he finished off. That was when I stuck up my hand.

"Yes, Daisy?" Polly's used to me interrupting.

"Do you know what the opera's about yet?" I asked. We were all dying to know.

"I'm afraid I don't, Daisy. Not really. But I do know that Mr Butterworth will be coming to school to talk to the choir, and he has sent us a song to be getting on with."

Well, that was something. It was a

Tuesday too, so later that morning our class had singing with Mrs Clinkscales.

When we went in, I walked straight over.

Mrs Clinkscales was sitting there like she always did – very relaxed and with her glasses stuck at the end of her nose. She dresses a bit strangely. Lots of bright colours, and sometimes her hair changes to match, too. Barry told us she was a traveller once, with an old bus and a load of dogs.

"Are we doing the opera song?" I asked Mrs Clinkscales.

Barry's mum smiled. "A bit later on I think, Daisy."

"All right, Year Five," said Miss Melrose. "Let's settle down, shall we?"

So that's what we did. I settled down next to Meggy, and she settled down next to Jimmy Black, worse luck.

"Right," Miss Melrose went on. "Now, let's begin with … what do you think Mrs

Clinkscales? *My Ship Sailed from China*?"
Barry's mum looked happy about that and
found the song in her music book.

And we were off.

*My ship sailed from China with a cargo
of tea,*

*All laden with treasures for you and for
me ...*

It's one of my favourite songs, so I always
give it lots of welly. I think it's something to
do with Barry's mum. It's not that she's a
brilliant piano player or anything, but she
just makes you want to let go. She sort of
bashes away and sways a bit and mouths the
words like she's having the best fun.

Of course, as I said, I was next but one to
Jimmy Black. Jimmy letting go at singing is a
bit scary-mary. He sounds like my dad's
shaver when the batteries go flat. Or a
bumblebee trapped in an oil drum. But he
was obviously enjoying himself. We all were,

12

so it was okay really.

"Well done everyone," said Miss Melrose, at the end.

So that was a good time to stick up a hand. "Can we do the opera now, Miss?"

"I don't see why not, Daisy. And actually, I believe Mrs Clinkscales knows the song well."

"That's right." Mrs Clinkscales smiled. "And so does Barry."

Barry hated being picked out by his mum, so he went a bit red.

"What's it called?" asked Meggy.

"It's called *Constant Billy*," said Mrs Clinkscales. "And it goes like this ...

*Constant Billy, my constant Billy, oh when will I see my Billy again?*

*When the fishes fly over the mountain, that's when I'll see my Billy again.*

*Billy again, Billy again, Billy again, Billy again.*

*When the fishes fly over the mountain,*
*that's when I'll see my Billy again."*

It didn't sound like opera. But it was bouncy, and you could tell how much Barry's mum liked it, which was a lot.

By the end of the morning, we all liked it. At least, we were singing it like we did.

"Right, Year Five," said Miss Melrose, "that all sounds wonderful, and I think Mrs Clinkscales will be playing the song for Year Six on Thursday?"

Barry's mum smiled to show that she would be.

"So," said Miss Melrose, "next Tuesday we'll all be joining together as the Flittering Primary School Choir. But for now it's a big thank you to Mrs Clinkscales, and can you all go back to the classroom quickly and quietly."

Well, I managed the quickly all right, but not the quietly.

"So how do you know *Constant Billy*?" I asked Barry.

"Just do," he said.

"Does your mum know anything about the opera?" Someone had to, surely?

"Not really."

So that was that. But I got the feeling that Barry knew a bit more than he was letting on.

# Chapter 3
# The Ghost Opera

In the end, can you believe it, we had to wait until Friday! That's when we finally found out, because Harvey Butterworth turned up at assembly. At the end of it all, Polly asked Years Five and Six to stay behind.

Then Harvey Butterworth stood up.

"Well," he said to us. "So this is the choir, then. And I expect you're all wondering about *Constant Billy*."

He'd got that right.

"The first thing to tell you is that *Constant Billy* is a community opera. So it's not like the opera you might hear in a grand theatre."

That meant Ravi's helmets and spears were out with the bin bags. Oh well.

"No," Harvey Butterworth went on, "it's going to be about some things that happened here in Flittering at the time of the First

World War. In those days, of course, the town was much, much smaller. More like a big village really, and like a lot of country places, Flittering had its very own team of Morris dancers."

Morris dancers! He really had said Morris dancers!

"I expect that some of you think Morris dancers are a bit un-cool. Something to make jokes about perhaps?"

Well, yes!

"But back in 1916, the Flittering Morris Men did something very brave. You see, they all joined the army and went off to France to fight in the terrible war. And just before the Battle of the Somme, while they were waiting for orders to attack, it's said that they danced *Constant Billy*. Some people think they even danced into battle."

Harvey Butterworth seemed to stop here and look around at our faces. So you can guess where my hand went.

"And what happened?" I asked.

"They were all shot down. Every one of them."

Wow!

"So our opera is going to tell their story and how the ghosts of the men came back to dance at Flittering Fair."

Cool. So it was like a ghost opera.

"Now, before I go," he said, "I'd like to hear you sing *Constant Billy*. I think you've been learning it with Mrs ... er ..."

"Mrs Clinkscales," I called out.

"Right, Mrs Clinkscales!" Harvey Butterworth sat down at the piano. "But today," he said with a smile, "you'll have to make do with my playing."

So we did. It wasn't a problem.

*Constant Billy, my constant Billy ...*

I thought it sounded brilliant, especially with Year Six as well, and I noticed that Harvey Butterworth's soppy smile had turned into a big grin.

Well, you can guess what my horrible brother thought.

"Morris dancing!" he sniggered. "Your stupid opera's about a bunch of men prancing about with hankies and bells! That's not just boring. That's totally sad and boring!"

"You wouldn't say that if you'd heard Harvey explain what happened and ... and ... how we're going to make it all come alive!" I protested.

"Oooooh," said Jamie, "so it's Harvey is it?"

"I hate you!" I shouted.

Luckily, Dad walked in on us. "Okay, okay, okay," he said. "What's going on?"

"Daisy's opera's all about Morris dancing!"

"No it's not, Dad. It's about the Flittering Morris Men and how they got killed in the War!"

"Oh, really? Well that's interesting." Dad sounded like he meant it, too. "I wonder if Buzz is involved?"

"Who's Buzz?"

"You know, Buzz Clinkscales. His boy's in your class."

"You mean Barry?"

"That's right."

"So why would Barry's dad be involved?"

"Oh, didn't you know?" said Dad. "Buzz is a Morris Man."

You should have seen the look on my brother's face. I don't know how I stopped myself from having a go at him. I ought to get some kind of medal.

# Chapter 4
# Enter Mrs Burlington

It was just like Miss Melrose had said. Year Six joined us for Tuesday singing. Now we were the Flittering Primary School Choir.

That morning, Barry's mum was dressed in velvety green and cottony purple. She'd put a streak in her hair, too. But there was someone else in the hall. Someone new. She was quite a big woman, and she was wearing a posh outfit. Meggy thought it was silk.

"Now children," said Miss Melrose. "This is Mrs Burlington, who has very kindly offered to help our choir. Mrs Burlington, you see, is a professional singer."

Miss Melrose smiled at Mrs Burlington and Mrs Burlington smiled at Miss Melrose. It was all very smiley. Except for Mrs Clinkscales. She wasn't smiling, but I didn't know why.

"And so," Miss Melrose went on, "I'll hand you over to Mrs Burlington."

"Why thank you, Miss Melrose," said our new leader. Then she looked around the hall and smiled at us. "Well boys and girls, isn't it marvellous that our school choir will be singing in Harvey Butterworth's opera? He really is a very important composer you know, and it's rather an honour for us to be working with him."

I wondered where the *us* had come from?

She hadn't finished either. "So we must try very hard to do the best job we can!"

*We?*

"Mrs Clinkscales," she went on, "do you think you could play *Constant Billy* for us. I'd rather like to hear the choir sing."

Barry's mum seemed okay about that, so she swivelled around on her seat and got herself ready. "All right, everyone?" she asked us.

And we were off.

*Constant Billy, my constant Billy ...*

*... that's when I'll see my Billy again.*

"That was marvellous!" said Mrs
Burlington. "But let's try it again, shall we?
And this time can I have everyone standing?"

So we did that.

*Constant Billy ...*

It sounded just the same to me.

*... Billy again.*

"Much, much, much better," said Mrs
Burlington. "So that's a very good start
indeed. But let me show you one or
two things."

Then she opened her mouth and
sang this big, huge,
long, loud note.

At playtime, Mrs Burlington was the
big gossip.

"Well," said Meggy, "what about her
voice? Wasn't it amazing? Maybe she's a diva
– like in the proper operas with the cow-
horns."

Meggy was right, because her voice really
was HUGE. "If we all sing like that," I said,
"I bet we'll blow the windows out."

Then I spotted Barry. "Hey, Barry!"

He came over.

"So what about your mum?" Meggy asked Barry.

"Yeah," I added. "How does she feel about Mrs Burlington coming in like she did?"

"Well," said Barry, "I think she feels a bit ..."

"What?"

"Like ... taken over, I suppose."

Well, I'd wondered about that myself, because I'd noticed that Barry's mum had looked a bit put out.

"Anyway," said Ravi, "I think your mum's the best!"

"Thanks," said Barry.

"What about your dad?" I asked. "Is he dancing in the opera?"

Barry seemed surprised. "How d'you know that?"

"Aha!" Meggy tapped the side of her nose. "We have our spies!"

# Chapter 5
## Scales and Exercises

On Friday, Polly told us the choir would be singing later that afternoon, because that was easiest for Mrs Burlington.

"So what about Mrs Clinkscales?" I asked Meggy as we walked out of the hall. "Is it easiest for her?"

Meggy just shrugged, but she got my point.

When choir practice came along, I decided I'd be especially nice to Barry's mum.

But I never got the chance, because she wasn't even there.

"What's happened?" I whispered to Barry.

"I dunno."

Mrs Burlington was there all right — wearing a smart grey suit and looking all I'm-in-charge-of-everything. But there was no sign of Mrs Clinkscales at all, and sitting at the piano was a tall, thin, weedy-looking man.

"Mrs Clinkscales can't join us today, so I want to introduce you to Geoffrey," said Mrs Burlington.

Geoffrey gave us all a weedy grin.

"Before we begin our songs," said Mrs Burlington, "I want to try some exercises with you."

Exercises? I didn't like the sound of exercises.

"Geoffrey's going to play a fcw notes and I want you to sing them back to me. So let's have everyone standing ..."

The next hour was just awful.

"We had singing today," I told my dad that evening.

"Not that again!" said Jamie. He'd heard it all earlier when I'd told Mum.

"Well, you can clear off then!" I shouted.

"Okay, I will." And he did. Hooray.

Dad sat down at the table. "So Daisy ... how was it?"

"Barry's mum wasn't there and Mrs Burlington made it like a horrible exam, but worse. We had to sing exercises and then she put us into groups and we had to sing scales. She put Meggy in a group with Jimmy Black and Vicky Price. She even kept them back at the end and told them they had to work especially hard. She was so patronising. I just hated it. It wasn't any fun at all."

"Oh dear," said Dad.

After tea, I met Meggy by the river. She had some bad news for me, too.

"I've decided," she said. "I'm giving up choir."

"You can't! You'll miss out on the opera!"

"I don't care! Mrs Burlington made me feel rubbish, like I wasn't wanted."

"But you are wanted! I want you! It won't be the same if you leave. And anyway, Meggy, you're not rubbish. No way!"

"So why did she put me in the losers' group?"

"Meggy, you are not a loser!"

"Oh yeah? Tell that to Old Burly!"

"Who?"

"Mrs Burlington."

Old Burly! I liked that a lot.

"Well if you go," I told Meggy, "then so will I!"

"Daisy!"

"I'll tell you what then," I said, "let's wait until Mrs Clinkscales comes back and see if things get back to normal, because I bet they will."

Meggy thought about that for a bit. "Well, okay," she said.

# Chapter 6
# Grand Snotties

That Saturday was Flittering Fair. It's not like a funfair with noisy music and candy-floss and moody boys who jump on the back of your dodgem and steer it for you. But it is fun. It's a sort of big fête mixed with a street party, and it's been going forever. It's probably the fair that Harvey Butterworth has in his opera.

Anyway, that afternoon I went along with Meggy.

We were wandering about when Meggy said, "Hey, look. One of those might be Barry's dad."

I could see what she meant, because over by the hot dog tent were some Morris dancers. They looked like cricketers wearing black boots. They had little bells tied below their knees and across their chests were thin sashes, like we wore for rounders.

"I reckon he's the one with the earring," I said.

"Yeah," said Meggy. "He does look like he could be."

"Shall we watch them dance?"

"All right, but when d'you think they'll start?"

"Well," I said, "let's ask Barry." I'd spotted him by the sponge-chucking stall.

"Hey, Barry," I called as we walked across.

It turned out we'd missed the dancing, but, yes, his dad did wear an earring.

Then Meggy asked her question. "How's your mum?"

"She's okay."

"So when's she coming back to play for us?"

That's when Barry told us. "She isn't."

What! It felt like a wet sponge had hit me in the face. "Why not?" I asked.

"She's had a big row with Mrs Burlington."

"What?"

"When?"

"Yesterday morning. After I'd left for school. Mrs Burlington rang my mum at home."

"And?"

"And she asked Mum if she'd come in and play all those arpeggios and scales. But Mum didn't want to. Mum said that stuff was all too serious and we should just sing the songs. So Mrs Burlington said she knew what she was doing, because she was a proper singer, and she'd find another piano player easily."

"Geoffrey."

"Exactly."

"But that's not right. Your mum should tell Miss Melrose or Polly."

"The trouble is," said Barry, "she doesn't want to get into an argument. She said that when she was on the road, she was always having fights with Mrs Burlington types. She calls them Grand Snotties. Mum says they always act as if they own everything, even the common land and the pathways. Mum says the travellers always lost out, in the end. So she doesn't want to go through it all again, not with Dad dancing in the opera."

"And you in the choir," I added.

"Right," said Barry, "and Mum says I should stick with it."

"Well, good."

"But I don't want to."

"Me neither," said Meggy. "Not now."

Well, I wasn't having that. "Come on," I said. "If we all stick with it we might find a way to make things right again!"

"Oh yeah?" said Barry. "How?"

"Yeah," agreed Meggy. "How?"

"Well ..."

"Yes?"

"Well ... we could have a petition! We could take it to Polly. What d'you think, Barry?"

"I dunno," he said. "I bet he'd ignore it. My mum says that's what happens with petitions. She always says if you want to get noticed, you have to get awkward."

Well, I thought about that for a moment, and then it came to me.

"We could go on strike!"

"What?"

"We could go on strike!" I repeated. "We could all refuse to sing. The whole choir. And we could demand that Barry's mum comes back! I bet that's what everyone wants, and I bet it would work, too, if we all stick together."

Meggy shrugged and Barry shuffled.

"Well?" I said.

"You're mad," said Meggy. But I could tell she liked the idea.

# Chapter 7
# On Strike

In the end, we decided to 'canvas opinion'. It's what my dad says, and it means finding out what everyone thinks.

One girl called Harriet Smith actually liked the arpeggios and scales! But she did play cello in an orchestra, so she was used to all that stuff. Mostly though, everyone agreed – Old Burly and her weedy Geoffrey were not a lot of fun, and the sooner Mrs Clinkscales came back, the better we'd like it.

"So what happens now?" asked Barry.

It was Thursday playtime and we were talking tactics.

"We wait until tomorrow morning and we tell everyone there's going to be a strike. And no one must sing a note."

"Just like that?" said Meggy.

"Exactly. And we act as if everyone has

agreed, so if anyone backs out or tells a teacher … then they're worse than a worm."

"Well, I hope it works," said Barry.

"Me too," said Meggy.

"Of course it will!" I told them. But I had my fingers crossed.

"Tomorrow, then," said Barry.

The next morning, Meggy, Barry and I had a very busy time.

"This afternoon!" said Ravi. "Wicked!"

"You're up for it, then?" I asked. He said he was. And so did everyone else. Well, everyone except Harriet Smith, who'd gone to have a brace fitted that morning.

"Come along, come along," said Old Burly when we all shuffled into the hall. "We haven't got all day."

I wondered if she'd pick up on our mood or anything. There was a lot of muttering and nudging going on.

"Goodness, choir," she said, "what is the matter?"

I bit my lip.

Then, Vicky Price started giggling.

Old Burly was so irritated. "Is there something funny?" she snapped. Vicky's giggles can be very catching. "This isn't some kind of joke, you know! Would you rather spend the afternoon outside Mr Pollard's office, Vicky?"

"No," said Vicky. "Sorry."

"I should think so!" said Old Burly, strictly. "Now, everyone settle down. Please! Right, choir," she said, "I want you all in your singing groups. So hurry up. Quick as you can, please."

"Just stay with me," I told Meggy. "She won't notice."

"Now, choir," Old Burly told us, "Geoffrey's going to play us a scale and I want you to

sing the notes back to me, as we
practised before."

Then she nodded to Geoffrey, and he
played the little scale.

Old Burly held up her hand and looked
around the room.

I held my breath.

"After the count of two," she said, "One ...
and two ..."

La ... la ... la!

Well, it was just brilliant, because the
whole school choir – THE WHOLE SCHOOL
CHOIR – was Harriet Smith! The rest of us

just stood there in silence. And Harriet
stopped after three notes!

"Goodness, choir!" said Old Burly, taken
aback. "Now come along! We have a lot of
work to do. So let me hear you ... ONE ...
AND TWO ..."

This time, even Harriet kept it zipped.

I wish you could have seen Old Burly's
expression.

"WHAT ON EARTH IS GOING ON?" she
demanded, turning beetroot.

43

No one said a thing. But when I looked around I realised why. Everyone was looking at me!

ME!

So I swallowed hard and stuck up my hand.

"It's a strike," I said. "I mean we're on strike ... the choir is."

"You're on WHAT?"

"The thing is," I swallowed again, "we want to sing songs like we used to and ..."

Old Burly turned to the piano. "Geoffrey," she said coldly, "can you take charge, please?"

Geoffrey gave her a weedy grin and Old Burly stormed out of the hall.

"Wow!" said Barry.

I knew I was in trouble.

Polly was pacing around his office when we went in.

"Ah, Mrs Dawes," he said to my mum. "Please sit down."

So Mum did. "I'd like Daisy to be here, if that's all right," she said.

Polly looked at me. "Of course."

Well, you can guess what happened. I got thrown out of the choir, didn't I?

# Chapter 8
# The Outcasts

"No way!" said Meggy.

"What about us?" said Barry. "It wasn't just you. It was us as well."

I just shrugged.

"That's it," said Meggy. "I'm out of it now. Definitely!"

"Me too," said Barry.

This time I didn't argue.

"So what did Polly say?" asked Barry.

"He said that Old Burly had his full backing, and we should be grateful to her because Harvey Butterworth was such a big composer, and Old Burly was helping the choir reach its potential."

"And what about my mum?" said Barry.

"Yeah!" said Meggy. "What did he say about Barry's mum?"

"Polly said he understood that she'd

agreed to it all. He even made it sound like your mum had let us down."

Barry and Meggy just stared at me.

"No," I said. "I couldn't believe it either."

At the next practice, Polly told the choir that the strike had been a silly mistake and they should put it all behind them. And – can you believe it – the wimps went along with it!

I'm just glad I wasn't there to hear it.

Nor were Meggy and Barry, because now we were out of the choir, we were told to stay in the classroom and keep ourselves busy. Twice a week, too, because Old Burly had the choir singing on Wednesdays as well as on Fridays.

Mostly, of course, us keeping busy meant us nattering about different things.

Like on Friday, it was about being a traveller in an old bus.

"So, what's it like?" Meggy wanted to know.

"Well, I was never on the road," explained Barry. "Not properly. Not like Mum and Dad were. But after I was born they still went round the summer festivals."

"Like Glastonbury?"

"Yeah, I think so. Of course there's lots I can't remember. But I can remember camping near Stonehenge, and the great big bonfire we had, and pulling black potatoes from the hot ashes."

"So how did you pay for food and things like petrol and clothes?" I asked.

"Mum and Dad had a pancake stall."

"Cool." I liked that idea a lot.

"Not just sugary pancakes either," said Barry. "They did savoury ones too, with fried eggs in the middle."

48

Well, I wasn't so sure about that, but I didn't say so. Anyway, that was when the door swung open and in walked Jimmy Black, Melanie Cheng, Robbie Watts and Vicky Price.

"What's happened?" I asked them. "What are you doing here?"

"We knew she didn't want us in her precious choir," said Jimmy, "so we said we wanted out."

"And she was obviously really pleased," said Melanie.

"She didn't even try to hide it!"

"I think that's best for all of us. That's what she said."

I could just imagine her snobby expression, too.

So that's how it was. The three of us turned into seven. We were the Constant Billy Outcasts.

"Well, you're better off in here," said Meggy defiantly.

We all agreed that Meggy was right, but it was still unfair, especially for Barry. I mean, it was his mum who'd been stomped on as if she didn't count.

# Chapter 9
# The Flittering Morris Men

That weekend, I finally got to see the Flittering Morris Men do their stuff. Barry said his dad was dancing at the Fox and Duck, so Meggy and I went along to check them out.

We found them all in the pub garden, getting ready. They looked just the same as before – all white, red and green.

Barry was there too, and so was his mum. They were sitting outside the pub, sipping drinks.

"Hello, Mrs Clinkscales," I said.

She was obviously pleased to see us. "Daisy and Megan! Barry's been telling me about your struggles, and I just want to say how touched I am that ..."

"Mum!" said Barry, butting in. He went a bit red, too.

Then Mrs Clinkscales nodded across to the Morris Men. One of them in a top hat was squeezing his concertina, and one with a big tambourine was banging out a rhythm.

"You're just in time," she said.

Well, I'm glad my horrible brother wasn't there, because Barry's dad and his Morris Men did look totally dippy. I mean, they were waving these hankies and skipping about. But even so, I quite liked the music, and, in a way their dancing reminded me of our singing before Old Burly arrived. Like they

52

were just letting go and didn't care.

"This next one's *Constant Billy*," said Barry.

Well, that got me interested – especially when the dancers stuffed away their hankies and picked up big, heavy sticks.

For the next few minutes, the Morris Men jumped about smashing the sticks together. And I mean SMASH! It was great fun to watch them. I almost started singing the words, too.

All the same, I wouldn't be telling Jamie about it later.

# Chapter 10
# The Crescendo

It was Ravi who told us the gossip.

"Harvey Butterworth's coming in on Wednesday and we're going to sing for him. Mrs Burlington says we have to show him how we've improved."

Ravi knew he'd said the wrong thing. Especially with Barry standing there, but I let him have it anyway.

"You mean now she's got rid of the dross and the losers?"

"No ... er ... what I mean is ..."

"It's all right, Ravi," said Barry. "We know what you mean."

To be honest, from the bits of singing we'd heard, the choir was sounding different. Harriet Smith was the star performer. We just didn't think that different meant better.

Robbie Watts was ill on Wednesday, so

there were six of us being outcasts. We were trying to ignore Old Burly's big show-off moment.

"I still like sugar and lemon," said Meggy, loudly.

Jimmy didn't agree. "Chocolate for me," he said. "But nice and runny."

We were talking pancakes, but it was still hard to blot out the singing. Especially when the song was *Constant Billy*.

"What d'you think he'll say?" I asked, meaning Harvey Butterworth. He was out in the hall with the choir.

"Well, I hope he hates it," said Meggy.

"But he won't, will he?" said Barry. "I bet he mixes with people like Old Burly all the time. I bet he likes all that complicated stuff she goes on about."

Then we heard the choir get louder and louder.

"That's the crescendo," said Melanie.

"They must be nearly finished."

Suddenly, the singing stopped dead, and all we could hear was a tiny bit of clapping.

"I hate singing," said Jimmy.

"Me too," said Vicky.

But they hadn't when Barry's mum played for us. Suddenly, my chest felt tight and I had a stinging feeling behind my eyes. I felt so angry! It was all so unfair. I wanted to rush into the hall and tell them just what I thought.

But of course I didn't.

It was just as well too, because right then we heard voices outside the classroom door.

"Shhh," said Meggy. "Listen!"

So we did.

It sounded like Old Burly, Polly and Harvey Butterworth.

"I'm so pleased you can hear the difference," said Old Burly smugly.

"Well, yes I can," said Harvey Butterworth.

"We've been very fortunate to have Mrs Burlington's help," said Polly.

"A little discipline and a little training," Old Burly went on, "that's all it takes. And I'm very happy to have played my part."

"Well ... er ... thank you," said Harvey Butterworth. Then he coughed. "But, tell me Mr Pollard, what happened to Mrs Clinkscales?"

"Oh yes, Mrs Clinkscales," said Polly. "I'm afraid she rather backed out of things."

I looked at Barry's face. I knew just what he was thinking.

"Well that's a shame," said Harvey Butterworth.

"Yes, isn't it?" said Old Burly, like it was nothing to do with her at all. "But then again, Geoffrey is so much more professional."

Harvey Butterworth did another little cough. "Of course, I'm sure you're right about that, Mrs Burlington."

"Call me Penelope."

Penelope! Well, she'd always be Old Burly to me.

"But you see ... Penelope ... I rather liked the way the children were singing when Mrs Clinkscales was playing for them. They sounded, well, like a roomful of children ... very natural."

"Excuse me," said Old Burly, "but is there something wrong with what I've achieved?" She sounded really huffy.

"Oh ... well ... no ... not wrong. No." said Harvey Butterworth. He was obviously embarrassed.

"I'm very pleased to hear it. And if you'll excuse me ... I feel I ought to get back to the choir."

"Oh ... right," said Harvey Butterworth.

"So, shall I see you on Friday afternoon then ... at half-past one?"

"Er ... yes ... of course."

"Excellent!" said Old Burly.

And we heard her marching off.

That was when I turned to Meggy. "I really hate her," I admitted. "She's just a great big bully."

"Shhh," whispered Meggy. "They're still talking."

"Oh dear," Harvey Butterworth said to Polly. "I seem to have really upset Mrs Burlington."

"I'm sure it's fine," said Polly. "Come on, let me show you out."

I looked across to Barry again. His fists were all clenched and blotchy white. "I'm going to tell him," he muttered. "I'm going to tell Polly what really happened."

But I had another idea, and no time to explain it, because right then I had to catch Harvey Butterworth.

"If anyone comes in," I said, "tell them I've gone to the toilet."

# Chapter 11
## Same as Always

"D'you think it'll work?" asked Meggy.

"Of course it will!" I said.

We found a table near the window, because that way we could keep an eye on the school gates.

"If you want," said Barry, "you can start your sarnies."

"No, it's all right," I said. "I don't want to be munching a mouthful. Not when it all kicks off."

Assuming it would kick off.

"Me neither," agreed Meggy.

So we kept our lunch-boxes closed, and our eyes open. I had a quick look at the clock. It was nearly ten to one.

"There she is!" said Barry.

He meant his mum of course. Mrs Clinkscales was walking through the gates.

"You may have to stall her for a bit," I said to Barry.

A few seconds later, Mrs Clinkscales popped her head through the swing doors, spotted us sitting there, and waved across.

We all went over and said hello.

"Oh, hi," she said, holding up the lunch-box. "You forgot this again. If I had a pound for every time …"

"Oh – thanks Mum," he said.

Mrs Clinkscales smiled. "Well, I'll be off then."

I gave Barry a tiny nudge.

"Um … can I just show you something, Mum? It's in the er … classroom."

"Well, of course. What is it?"

"Oh, it's just … you know, something I want to show you."

"Right," said Mrs Clinkscales, but she did look a little bit puzzled.

The four of us went off to our classroom.

"Now … where is it?" said Barry. "I know it's here somewhere …"

It wasn't a bad performance, actually. But, even so, his mum was beginning to wonder.

"What's going on?" she said. "Is there something I should …"

"It's all right!" I interrupted. "He's here! He's coming through the gates."

"Who's here?" asked Mrs Clinkscales.

"Come on," said Barry, and he grabbed his mum's sleeve.

We caught him in the corridor.

"Ah," he said. "Not late am I?"

"Oh no," I said, "You're bang on time. Actually, there's someone we want you to meet … this is Mrs Clinkscales."

"Oh," he said, looking at Barry's mum, "Well I'm Harvey Butterworth, and I'm very pleased to meet you."

Well, it was exactly like I thought. They got on brilliantly! Barry's mum told Harvey about everything that had been going on.

"Good grief!" he said. "I wish I'd known all this before."

"See," I whispered to Barry. "I told you!"

Then Meggy prodded my arm. "Look who's coming now!" she said.

It was Old Burly. With weedy Geoffrey two steps behind.

"Excuse me," she boomed, "but is there something going on here?"

"Ah, hello Penelope," said Harvey Butterworth.

The rest of us just stood there. But Old Burly totally ignored us anyway and marched straight up to Harvey. "I hope there's no problem," she said bossily.

But this time he wasn't going to be bullied. "None at all," he said. "Everything's just fine."

Old Burly didn't like that answer one bit. "Oh, really?"

"The thing is," said Harvey Butterworth, "I'm rather hoping Mrs Clinkscales will come back and play piano for us."

Barry looked at his mum and grinned.

"Oh no, no," said Old Burly. "I'm sorry, Harvey, but that won't do at all. I can't possibly manage without Geoffrey. Not now."

Geoffrey gave us his weedy grin.

"I understand that," said Harvey Butterworth, "but, well, that's rather the thing, isn't it? You see, I don't want to seem ungrateful to you and Geoffrey, but, how can I put it ..."

Suddenly Old Burly went totally white. "You mean ... I'm not ... not wanted?"

"Well, I wouldn't put it like that, Penelope. It's more that your particular skills aren't really in tune with the needs of our opera."

"And ... and ... and her's are?" Old Burly gasped, pointing at Barry's mum.

"Well, yes," said Harvey Butterworth.

"Actually, they are." Then he turned to Barry's mum. "So what do you say?" he asked her.

Mrs Clinkscales smiled. "Well of course, I'd be delighted to play for the choir."

Old Burly just stared. She wasn't used to this sort of treatment at all.

It was Geoffrey who opened his mouth next. "Well ... er ... good luck then," he said nervously, and with a weedy grin.

"Geoffrey!" said Old Burly, as if he'd totally let her down. Then she gave Barry's mum a really nasty look and said, "We'll see what Mr Pollard has to say about this!" And she stormed off to find him, a bit like a rhinoceros having a really, really bad day.

"Er, sorry," said Geoffrey, and he tripped along after her.

But Harvey didn't look the least bit worried. Not now Barry's mum was coming back. "It's going to be just fine," he said.

Well, Polly's timing was perfect, because that was when he appeared from out of nowhere. "Is everything all right?" he asked.

"Oh yes, Sir," I said.

"Everything's definitely all right," said Barry.

"But there is someone looking for you," added Meggy.

And we all grinned. Poor old Polly!

"You three!" said Mrs Clinkscales. "You set it all up, didn't you?"

We were walking home after school. I felt like skipping.

"It was Daisy's idea," said Meggy. "She thought if you and Harvey Butterworth could just get together before Mrs Burlington arrived, everything would sort itself out."

"He so obviously agreed with you," I explained, "about singing being fun and everything. And once he found out what really happened, we knew he'd want you to come back."

Mrs Clinkscales smiled. "So, accidentally," she said, "Barry forgot his lunch."

"I knew you'd bring it in!" said Barry.

"And we knew that Harvey would be here early, because Daisy had told him a little white lie."

"So," I said, "that's one up for the travellers, then!"

Barry's mum seemed surprised at first, but then she just grinned. "That's right, Daisy. One up for the travellers!"

"When are you coming in again?" asked Meggy.

"On Tuesday, Megan. Same as always."

That's exactly what I wanted to hear – same as always.

# Chapter 12
# The Last Night of the Opera

Singing in the opera was amazing.

Our choir stood at the side of the stage.
While we were singing, Barry's dad and the
Flittering Morris Men did their weird ghost
dance. It was so spooky, because all the
jumping about was just the same as before,
but this time they were barefoot and bloody.
They were totally silent too – even when they
smashed their sticks together. I bet it took
ages to practise.

After the show, Harvey made a speech.

"And a big thank you to Hilary Clinkscales," he said, "because without her help, the school choir could never have sounded so wonderful. Hilary certainly has that special gift of making music fun."

Well, that's how we all felt.

It was the next weekend, and Barry's mum was making us pancakes with fried eggs in the middle. Meggy had brought along the cards.

"So," said Barry, "it's called *Happy Families* because we have to collect the families into sets, right?"

"Well, normally," said Meggy, "but Daisy has some different rules."

"You see, Barry," I said, "there's something I think you need to know about Mrs Bun and Dr Bones ..."